YONDER'S HENRY

BY

THORNE SMITH

Copyright © 2013 Read Books Ltd.
This book is copyright and may not be
reproduced or copied in any way without
the express permission of the publisher in writing

British Library Cataloguing-in-Publication Data
A catalogue record for this book is available from the
British Library

Contents

Thorne Smith 1

Yonder's Henry

I 5

II 7

III 10

IV 18

Thorne Smith

James Thorne Smith Jr. was born at the U.S. Naval Academy in Annapolis, Maryland in 1892. His mother died when he was young, and he spent the early portion of his life in the care of various aunts across the American South. It was during his time in North Carolina that Smith began to tell his first stories and poems, to his cousin and his dog. Smith spent his teens at military academies, where he was an average student who enjoyed his English classes but little else, and eventually graduated in 1910 at the age of eighteen.

After leaving college, Thorne took a job in a New York advertising agency and wrote copy for Dr. Lyon's Tooth Powder. In 1917, following in the footsteps of his father – a semi-famous Commodore – he enlisted in the US navy. While serving, he became editor of *The Broadside*, a magazine for Naval Reserve personnel, and his short stories proved a big hit among the servicemen (they would later be reprinted, selling more than 70,000 copies). Five years after being discharged from the Navy in 1919, Thorne gave up his job in advertising – an industry he despised, but which he continually fell back on in order to make money – to devote himself full-time to writing. In 1926, he published the novel that made his name: *Topper: An Improbable Adventure*. A comedy fantasy novel about a respectable banker called Cosmo Topper and his misadventures with a couple of ghosts, Marion and George Kerby, *Topper* was a great success. In 1937, MGM adapted it into a film, with Cary Grant playing George Kerby. Smith eventually wrote a three-book *Topper* series, all of which were adapted into films, as well as a 78 episode television series.

Smith published ten more novels during the rest of his life (including the other two of the *Topper* trilogy), his most ambitious of which was *Dream's End* (1927), a florid, serious Gothic romance featuring heavily symbolic dreams. However, Smith was undoubtedly best known for his humorous works. Indeed, although somewhat neglected now, Smith is regarded by critics as one of the top writers of American comic fiction to come out of the twenties. He died of a heart attack in 1934 while on holiday in Florida, aged just 42.

Yonder's Henry

A slightly befuddled account of a completely cockeyed hunt, starring Henry, a foxy hound

by

Thorne Smith

YONDER'S HENRY

I

His question so upset me I put down my drink untasted.

Albert was like that. Upsetting. Years ago I had gone to school with Albert. He had been upsetting then - a sort of experimental liar indefatigable in his efforts to plumb the depths of human credulity. Fifteen years in the discard that had been. Now fate had returned Albert - Albert Green - to my side. In a little bar in a little town in the large state of Texas we had been celebrating all morning. I now wonder why. In his charmingly casual manner Albert had just inquired if I cared to go fox hunting. He had added modestly that he lived in this state of Texas together with a population composed almost entirely of foxes. The first part of this statement might just possibly be true. I'm inclined to believe it is. He seemed to be living in Texas. It would take a big, strong state like Texas to stand for Albert. He would have upset any normal state just as he upset me. At the moment he was more interested in upsetting a lot of foxes.

I asked him a frank question. "Albert," I asked him, "do I bear on my face the stamp of a man consumed with a secret passion for foxes?"

"Don't have to be passionate about foxes, just to hunt 'em," he replied. "In fact, you can hate foxes."

I stopped to consider exactly where I stood about foxes. It surprised me to discover that I had no strong feelings either for or against foxes. Years ago I had heard something about a fox mentioned in connection with a bunch of grapes. Since that time, however, foxes had gone their way and I had gone mine. Our paths never crossed. I saw no reason why they should.

"We'll waive that part of it," I said with befitting dignity. "What do you know about fox-hunting anyway?"

Albert indulged in a tragic laugh. "Every possible thing," he asserted. "Own the finest pack of hounds in Texas. You'd think they were on tracks the way they follow foxes. Wonderful dogs. And Henry! What a hound. Man! Man! Ho, I know all about foxes. Recognize one at a glance."

"To recognize a fox is one thing," I told him, "but to chase him over the landscape is an elk of another burrow."

"Come on down to my place and I'll show you," urged Albert. "We'll do more than just hunt foxes. Henry'll juggle some for you. It's his way."

Precocious dogs, like precocious children had always been one of my pet aversions, but the picture of a noble hound juggling a number of foxes fired my imagination. I accepted Albert's invitation, which goes to prove that one should never talk with Albert in a barroom.

On further consideration I am inclined to believe one should never talk with Albert at all.

II

After sleeping through numerous miles of Texas scenery while Albert sat alone with his God and his automobile, I found myself gazing miserably into the grim but good looking face of Mrs. Albert across the sparkling reaches of her luncheon table.

"The trouble with you boys," she said, "is that you don't drink enough."

Suiting her action to her words she replenished our glasses with what she was pleased to call real Texas mule, adding that it was something like hair of the dog that had so brutally and recently mutilated us.

"My dear," remarked Albert, accepting the drink, but ignoring the remark that went with it. "I've decided to hold the fox hunt tomorrow - you know, the regular weekly fox hunt."

"Yes," I added. "He wants to show me Henry in action. I can see him now at the head of your splendid pack of hounds."

Mrs. Albert considered the suggestion. She poured out a drink for herself and tossed it off with professional detachment.

"Can you?" she asked in level tones. "You must have a remarkable imagination. Most northerners would not even believe it."

"My wife is a little touchy about Henry," Albert hastened to explain. "I brag so much about him. Might as well hold the hunt tomorrow at the usual time."

"Oh certainly," replied Mrs. Albert. "Why not?" As she rose from the table she added, "Did I hear a door slam?"

"That's difficult to say," said Albert.

"Correct. It's almost impossible to tell whether a door has slammed or not after it's once slammed." Mrs. Albert continued thoughtfully. "It leaves no tracks behind."

"Not like Henry," I said to Albert. "He must fairly scoop up the earth when he once gets started."

I though I saw Albert flinch. "Of course," he agreed quite seriously. "Fairly excavates it, that dog."

"Come, Albert," said his wife. "We must see about that door...and make some arrangements for tomorrow."

"May I stroll out and take a look at the pack?" I inquired.

"I'd hardly advise it," observed Albert. "Not just before the hunt."

"No, don't do that," put in his wife. "Henry does much better after he's been lonely a spell."

Later that afternoon I inadvertently overheard Mrs. Albert at the telephone.

"Certainly," she was saying. "Bring your guests right along. We have an alcoholic with us who doesn't know the first thing about fox-hunting. Doubt if he knows one end of a horse from the other." She must have suspected my presence for she went on in an altered voice, "Oh, yes, he's quite charming, this guest of ours. You must meet him. And tell the others not to dress formally, you know. Cut out the red coats for a change. He hasn't an outfit with him. Neither have your guests, I reckon." When she had hung up she turned to me.

"Did you hear?" she asked.

"No I replied gallantly. "A door slammed. But I gathered I won't be alone in my misery."

"No," said Mrs. Albert. "There will be several other novices."

That night Albert, weak from the lack of liquor, came in to my room and deposited a bundle of clothing on a chair.

"For tomorrow," he explained, eyeing the garments with disfavor. "The hunt, you know."

"Oh, I don't care what I look like," I assured the dispirited man. "What I'm interested in is what Henry looks like. Does he usually juggle the foxes before or after the hunt?"

"It makes no difference to Henry," said Albert brightening. "Whenever he gets a fox. Some call it brutal."

"Nonsense," I replied heartily.

Albert went away.

III

When I looked out of my window the next morning I received a decided shock. For a moment I feared that Albert had gotten himself in some trouble. His ancestral home seemed to have become entirely surrounded either by bandits or deputies. I was not sure which. Anyway, they were rough looking men, most of them carrying shot guns and rifles while others were swinging large, ugly looking clubs. There were many women also. They had the rough and ready appearance of experienced camp followers.

"The hunt breakfast," Albert murmured over my shoulder. I gave a slight start. He had made his appearance so quietly. "The regular hunt breakfast," he repeated.

"Why, there's hardly a red coat on the lot," I complained. "Albert, I feel cheated."

"Seldom wear red coats except on formal occasions," said Albert. "Thought you knew that."

"What does it matter?" I said philosophically. "We're chiefly interested in foxes, after all."

"So we are," replied Albert simply. "What's the sense in a lot of red coats, anyway? I don't think the dogs like 'em or the foxes either."

"Don't see why they should," I told him. "But I will ask you this. Do you use clubs and rifles and machine guns on your damn Texas foxes?"

"Not machine guns," said Albert gently. "We use the others for hand to hand fighting. Texas foxes are often violent. They don't seem to understand."

"Neither do I, quite," I admitted. "Why don't you bomb the foxes and save yourself a lot of trouble?"

"That wouldn't be sporting," said Albert blandly. "and anyway, we like it. Then again, there's Henry to consider. He must have his foxes."

"That's so, too," I replied. "I guess that great beast would die unless he had his foxes."

"Those clubs and guns are brought along just in case," he informed me.

"In case of what?" I asked.

"Of wild turkeys," he answered with out cracking a smile.

When I had finished dressing I was nearly as funny looking as Albert, but not quite. However, I was funny looking enough. I was exactly as funny looking as an oversized pair of plus fours, a checked flannel shirt, high boots and a campaign hat could make me. Albert was a little funnier because he was wearing a pair of white duck trousers encased in knee-length leggins. His nautical appearance was somewhat nullified by the presence of a large floppy straw hat on the back of his head. A corduroy hunting jacket alone suggested the general nature of Albert's intentions. There was a colored shirt also which I find it pleasanter not to write about.

"The foxes are going to have the laugh of their lives today," I remarked when I had acclimated myself to Albert. "They'll be too weak to run."

"Come," said Albert with dignity. "The hunt breakfast is on. There is drink."

"Let's abandon this incessant fox hunting," I suggested, "and make millions on the stage. We wouldn't have to do much, Albert. One look would drive 'em frantic."

"Later, perhaps," replied Albert a little moodily. "We have to go through with this fox hunt first. Come on."

I was introduced to a series of majors, doctors and judges. All men over thirty seemed automatically to come into a title. Whether they were merely hunt breakfast titles or not I never learned. There was one rotund colonel, authentic in every detail, an upon him was bestowed all the honor and glory due to his colorful record of violent and abrupt endings. He was the Colonel. Fat was this gentleman, fat, pompous and over-blooded, but a life-loving soul withal. In his youth he had been the life of all the local lynching parties, and now, in his declining years, he had acquired the reputation of an implacable hunter. He was wearing a Prince Albert coat and highly polished boots which lent the only touch of distinction to this nondescript gathering.

After being properly introduced to the ladies, all of whom seemed to be guarding some shameful secret the full significance of which they failed to grasp themselves, I was placed by the side of my hostess, and urged to drink. She subjected me to one swift scrutiny, then quickly dropped her eyes.

"Pardon me," she said in a strained voice. "I think I heard a door slam."

The next moment she rose hastily and walked unsteadily toward the house. With pained eyes I followed her retreating figure.

Down the line a lady showing no end of well turned southern legs as she sat on the grass was speaking in an excited voice and waiving a cocktail glass in the air.

"What a lark," she proclaimed. "John's never so much as seen a fox and he can't stand the sight of horses. They give him a violent rash, do horses."

I turned and regarded my host inquiringly, "Is he one of the initiates like myself at this ceremony?" I asked.

"Yes," he answered. "There are several others - lots of new faces, in fact. You won't be alone. Drink up."

A man on my right leaned confidently over and made helpless, little motions with his hands.

"Pardon me," he said incredulously, "but do I understand we are actually going fox hunting?"

I told him that that was about the size of it.

"Fancy that," he observed musingly. "Of all things, fox hunting. Wonder where Mr. Green caught the beast. Haven't seen a fox in years. I'll ask him."

To my great delight he leaned over and made some more motions at Albert.

"Mr. Green," he whispered piercingly. "Where in the world did you get this fox?"

"What fox?" exclaimed Albert in a startled voice, looking quickly about as if he feared a fox was creeping up behind him.

"You know," said the man mysteriously. "This fox we're supposed to hunt."

"Certainly," I put in. "The fox Henry's going to juggle with several others."

"Who's Henry?" asked the man innocently.

"Why don't you know Henry?" I replied with some amazement. "He's the greatest foxer in the state of Texas, that dog."

"Strange," muttered the man. "Don't know him - but I'm a stranger to these parts."

"We raised many of our foxes in England," Albert explained.

"And ruin them in Texas," said the stranger.

Albert's answer was cut short by a sudden shout winging across the lawn from the direction of the outhouses. I looked up and saw a negro, running with great concentration; coming in our direction. He was leaning so far over in his efforts to separate himself from some still unrevealed peril that he gave the impression of a six-day bicycle racer. then something happened which I am sure must have come upon everybody as a complete surprise to put it mildly. Before our astonished eyes the negro was borne down and blotted out beneath an onrushing avalanche of dogs. The air was disturbed by eager yelpings and churned by innumerable jauntily waiving tails. In another moment the hunt breakfast had been reduced to a shambles. One imperishable vision of our colonel staunchly defending a chunk of fried chicken was vouchsafed me. Then he, too, disappeared, emulating the negro, as the dogs danced giddily over his recombent form. After that my impressions became somewhat clouded. I remember a large dog neatly removing a sandwich from my fingers and breathing appreciatively in my face. Sandwiches seemed to be moving through the air like things of life. The once spotless table cloth was leaping weirdly under the stress of greedily searching muzzles. Figures of men and women as they rolled and struggled on the grass were caught in the most undignified, not to say comprimising positions. The element of surprise was all in favor of the raiders. The famous hunt breakfast was theirs without a struggle. I remember hearing quite distinctly Mrs. albert as if lost to decency, ironically cheering the pack on to still greater endeavors. From their utterdisregard of all those little niceties of deportment that give life its subtle fragrance I decided that it had been many a long day since those dogs had enjoyed a square meal.

Then above the din and the barking, the cries of the insulted and injured and - I regret to say - the shocking blasphemy of out colonel, my host, Albert, who should have been master of this hunt, lifted up his voice in command.

"Grab sticks!" he shouted. "Grab anything and beat them off!"

Then began a grim struggle, man facing defiant beast, for the honor and supremacy of the human race. We fought those dogs bitterly and oftentimes unfairly. For example, I saw one gentleman deliberately enticing one of the enemy to accept a peace offering of chicken - a delicious bit it looked - and then when the poor animal had been betrayed by its oen greed this man, this southern gentleman, squared off and kicked the dog quite severely in the rump. Foot by foot the dogs yeilded and were driven backin the direction whence they came. One inspired sportsman accelerated their departure by firing off a shotgun. This horrid noise entirely demoralized the dogs, all of whom must have been born gun shy. With yelps of nervous alarm they sheathed their once valiant tails and deployed in the direction of the barn.

Mrs. Albert was sitting calmly on the grass. Her husband was rushing from one guest to another, assuring everyone that everything was all right, and begging them not to let this slight interruption mar the pleasure of the hunt.

"Pleasure?" one forthright gentleman - obviously a novice - demanded indignantly. "How did you get that way? You mean the horror of the hunt."

"What's the matter with you?" Mrs. Albert asked defensively before I had opened my lips. "There's nothing unusual about this hunt breakfast. Only last week the dogs broke loose and one of the fresh things had the nerve to snatch a cocktail right out of my hand. Think of that."

I did. I looked steadily at Mrs. Albert's innocently turned up face and thought of that as well as other things. This made me think of Albert, the last person in the world I wanted to think about at that moment.

IV

I was being introduced by Albert to the mount upon which I was to pursue foxes for the reminder of the day.

"This is Molly," he said with Jefersonian simplicity. "Your horse."

It had to be my horse because most certainly no one else would have taken Molly as a gift. As I studied this disillusioned featuresof this venerable wreck I feared that she was going to take advantage of her sex and weep on my shoulder. Nevertheless, I mounted to her back and awited with closed eyes the inevitable crash. Molly braced herself, quivered along her keel, but managed to remain erect.

The lawn now became the scene of fresh activity. The colonel, still dazed, with the help of three strong men was being elevated to the top of his horse, an operation in which neither the colonel nor the horse seemed to be the least bit interested. Presently the sweating huntsmen were safely if not securely installed in their saddles while the women stood about and made unhelpful but irritating suggestions, as women always do and always will when men are striving to maintain their dignity in the face of overwheling odds.

Once more the pack appeared. Its mood had now shifted from one of famished activity to satiated greed. Leisurely the hounds ambled across the lawn and slipped past us with many a futive backward glance, as if expecting a sudden kick. Their respective rumps were guiltily shrunken. Once safely out of reach they broke into a run and speedily absorbed themselves into the landscape, severalsecretly amused negroes pretending to pursue them.

"Are you all ready?" cried Albert, holding up his hand. "If you are, let's go."

"Just a minute now," came the querulous voice of the stranger. "Go where, Mr. Green? I've gotten me up on the top of this dumb beast like you said but damned if I enjoy the prospect of jouncing all over the countryside on it without any idea where I'm going or when I'm coming back."

In the face of this reasonable question the hunting party fell into a depressed silence. Obviously many of its members were asking themselves the same thing. Albert rushed gamely into the breach.

"We go wherever the fox goes," he explained.

"What fox?" demanded the man.

"I don't know what fox," said Albert. "Just any fox - the fox we're after."

"What's this fox gone and done, Albert" another unknown inquired mildly.

"He hasn't done anything," said my host.

"Then why are we after him?" continued the voice.

"Well, you can't very well have a fox hunt without some sort of fox, can you?" asked Albert bitterly. "It's all very simple. We just sit on our horses and go where the fox goes."

"If you think it's so simple sitting on this animated file,"someone indignantly observed, "I'd like you to change places with me and let him chafe you for awhile. I'm tow-thirds ruined already and we haven't even started yet."

"Let's hope this old fox goes to bed, then we can all do likewise," the weary stranger offered hopefully.

As the company straggled through the gate, a sudden cry of warning brought us to a stop. It seems that our colonel with the aid of a low-hanging limb had somehow managed to unhorse himself. Turning quickly, I caught a momentary glimpse of that stout gentleman decending earthward with terrific speed where he landed in a sitting position and remained as if atrophied. Horses and riders alike gazed down at him with concentrated attention as if wondering why their colonel had taken it into his head to act in such a peculiar manner.

"What's the meaning of all this?" asked Albert pushing his horse through the circle. The colonel regarded him balefully.

What the hell do you think it means?" he demaned in a high, thin voice. "That I'm playing mud pies?" Young man, it means foul play. I was struck from behind."

"Well," said Albert at last, "we can't very well leave him sitting there like that all day. Get him back on his horse and we'll make a fresh start."

The colonel accepted a drink and once more allowed himself to be heaved into the saddle, where he sat in stunned silence.

"I say, Mr. Green," a third stranger to Albert cried out, "What are we supposed to do with this fox once we catch him?"

"Which is very doubtful," the first one added.

Albert laughed with false heartiness. "Have your little joke," he called back.

"It's no joke," said the other earnestly. "Swear to God I wouldn't know how to act with a real live fox."

"Cut off his brush," grated Albert.

"His what?" came the startled rejoiner in a shocked voice. "Oh, Mr. Green."

"You know as well as I do," replied Albert.

"Oh," exclaimed the other. "You don't like to talk about it. I think I know know."

Albert flushed furiously.

"Say, Mr. Green," asked a rider rather plaintively. "Why are you so mean to foxes, anyway? You must certainly hate 'em to do a thing to'em - you know - like you said."

At this moment I reminded Albert that unless we looked for the dogs we might lose them forever, not that I greatly cared. A startled expression added to the unhappiness of his features. He held up a hand and listened.

"Now where do you rekon those dogs could have gotten themselves to?" he asked at last.

"Let's make it a dog hunt instead of a fox hunt," a bright young man suggested.

Albert wineed, then suddenly his face cleared. From far down the road came an awful sound. I had begun to doubt the existance of Henry, but now I changed my mind.

"Yonder's Henry!" exclaimed the delighted Albert with as much pride as if he were emitting all those terrible sounds himself." "Hear him!"

We did. Henry had a shocking voice.

"Glad I'm not a fox," someone piously observed. "I'm scared even to hunt with that dog lose."

"Henry's giving tounge," exclaimed Albert.

"Giving!" exclaimed the accurate rider. "Henry's doing heaps more than that. He's fairly tossing tongue away - lavishing tongue on the countryside."

When finally we found the dogs they were in various reposeful attitudes while they idly watched one of their members trying to get at a negro clinging to the topmost limb. This dog was beyond description. Canine obscenities gushed from its throat. Its fangs were bared and foam flecked its lips. Henry, without a doubt. Upon seeing Albert, the negro in the tree let out a yell.

"Fo' Gawd's sake, Mr. Albert, take dat dawk away or I'sa gone nigger."

Albert looked up at the negro, then transferred his attention to the frantic beast. "Josh," he said at last, "that dog isn't Henry. Where do you suppose he came from?"

"I don't care who the hell he is," one of our little group complained, "if he doesn't stop making those awful noises I'll climb one of those trees myself.

"No, suh," responded Josh. "Dat dog sho ain't no Henry. Dat dog's Fanny. Mr. Albert, Fanny's by the way of being a bloodhound. We sort of invited her over last night just to fancy up the pack a bit."

"A charming piece of garnishing, Fanny," remarked a gentleman on my left.

"Well, Josh," said Albert wearily, "I reckon you'd better get Fanny home or she'll be treeing every damn nigger in the countryside and then we'l never get any foxes.

"Foxes," I quietly inquired.

"Certainly," shot back Albert. "I said foxes. Henry must be looking for some now."

The subject was changed by a sudden groan from our colonel.

"Gentlemen," he announced, "I can stand it no longer. I fear I'm bleeding to death."

"Where?" demanded Albert, turning to cope with this new disaster.

The colonel seemed reluctant to take us into his confidence concerning the exact location of his mortal wound.

"I must have sat on my flask," he replied after some hesitation. "When I fell, you know. I've been sitting on the pieces ever since."

"My God," breathed Albert. "What next? Help the colonel down, some of you, and I'll see what I can do about it."

Our colonel asked Albert, now assuming the role of glass picker, retired among the bushes with old fashioned southern modesty. Presently Albert reappeared.

"I am happy to announce," he said, "that the colonel's injuries were more demeaning to a gentleman of his high spirit than serious to his person. He has decided to continue with us. Let us hope and pray that this will be the last interruption. We must now find Henry, leader of the pack."

An ironical cheer greeted this fine speech. The colonel was placed delicately on his horse. The negro attendants beat the dogs into a reluctant state of activity. Once more the hunt was in motion. For an hour or more we cantered along the roads pleasantly enough, stopping occasionally to let the pack catch up with us. The dogs were friendly, courteous and even playful. They seemed to nourish no grudge against us, but it was plain to see that no one had taken the trouble

Yonder's Henry

to tell them what it was all about. To the pack it was an outing - a casually informal affair.

"Just wait till they catch up with Henry," Albert kept assuring us. "then just watch 'em go."

We did. From somewhere far down the road the ravings of a mad dog were bourne to us. Albert's face became radiant.

"Yonder's Henry!" he shouted. "Hear him!"

The dogs, exerting their last ounce of energy, broke into a run and sped down the road. Fresh hope returned to our hearts as we thundered after. Perhaps there might be something to this fox-hunting business after all. The pack was now in full cry. We rounded a curve and saw the dogs streaming across an open field in the direction of some woods. A large and elated rabbit was cutting insulting capers in their faces. Albert's own face looked a trifle dismayed.

"Shucks," he said, "that fool rabbit just crossed the fox's trail, but he won't put Henry off. Follow on."

Follow on we did, and in short time crashed into the woods. Then consternation reigned. Close to my ear a shotgun suddenly exploded. It exploded very close to my ear.

"Moonshiners!" someone shouted, and the effect was electrifying.

From behind the most innocent looking trees bearded faces appeared. In a methodical manner the owners of these faces began to discharge lead into the ranks of the disorganized hunt. In an instant, dogs, horses and men were fighting democratically together for mere survival. There was a great thrashing of branches and a complicated entangling of man and beast. The moonshiners seemingly had an inexhaustable supply of ammunition and a passionate desire to use it. I now saw the reasonalbeness of our clubs and guns, although our party used neither.

Personally, I sustained no loss other than Molly and a large quantity of breath. From the safety of a slight elevation I observed the component parts of the hunt break from the woods and dash across the field. Men who had known each other for years passed without the slightest recognition, so occupied were they with their own thoughts. the field was dotted with horses, dogs and men, some of the men in their impatience even pushing horses out of their way. I felt that I was look at an old English hunting print suddenly thrown into reverse. Some of those dogs, I dare say, are still running.

The last to withdraw from the woods were our colonel, Albert and my Molly. The colonel was leaning on Albert's arm. Molly appeared to be trying to hold his other hand. I was joined by this little group and with Albert's help put our colonel on to Molly. He sat well forward and practiced soul stirring groans. Foxes would have little to fear from our colonel for many days to come. Very little was said. There was hardly anything either fit or safe to be said unless we talked about the weather. Albert steadily refused to meet my eyes.

After an interminable walk we at last approached the smooth green lawn of my host's home. Several members of the hunt were grouped round the rumpled tablecloth. They were looking down sadly on a large inert body. Mrs. Albert was saying things. We listened.

"Would you believe it?" she was saying. "Ever since you all got out of sight he's been sleeping there just like a lamb. Must have eaten too much hunt breakfast. Isn't he sweet?"

We, too, gazed down at the slumbering figure. The expression in Albert's eyes was too terrible for man to behold. I felt inclined to withdraw quietly to leave him alone with his sorrow. The figure, as if feeling our eyes upon it, feebly attempted to raise its head. Slumber overcame it. A gnawed chicken bone slipped from its mouth as it drifted off to sleep. A tail moved with propitiatory intentions. A gentle sigh fell upon the evening air.

The our colonel lifted up his voice.

"Yonder's Henry!" he howled, and then there was a touch of maddness in his eyes. "Hear him!" He paused, squared his shoulders, then confronted Albert.

The rest is silence...

www.ingramcontent.com/pod-product-compliance
Ingram Content Group UK Ltd.
Pitfield, Milton Keynes, MK11 3LW, UK
UKHW041303180426
11947UKWH00009B/642